-The Chronicles of-
Narnia
The Lion, The Witch and The Wardrobe

WALT DISNEY PICTURES AND WALDEN MEDIA PRESENT "THE CHRONICLES OF NARNIA: THE LION, THE WITCH AND THE WARDROBE" BASED ON THE BOOK BY C.S. LEWIS

A MARK JOHNSON PRODUCTION AN ANDREW ADAMSON FILM MUSIC COMPOSED BY HARRY GREGSON-WILLIAMS COSTUME DESIGNER ISIS MUSSENDEN EDITED BY SIM EVAN-JONES PRODUCTION DESIGNER ROGER FORD

DIRECTOR OF PHOTOGRAPHY DONALD M. McALPINE ASC, ACS CO-PRODUCER DOUGLAS GRESHAM EXECUTIVE PRODUCERS ANDREW ADAMSON PERRY MOORE

WALDEN MEDIA SCREENPLAY BY ANN PEACOCK AND ANDREW ADAMSON AND CHRISTOPHER MARKUS & STEPHEN McFEELY PRODUCED BY MARK JOHNSON PHILIP STEUER DIRECTED BY ANDREW ADAMSON Walt Disney Pictures

Distributed by BUENA VISTA PICTURES DISTRIBUTION. THE CHRONICLES OF NARNIA, NARNIA, and all book titles, characters and locales original thereto are trademarks of C.S. Lewis Pte Ltd. and are used with permission. ©Disney Enterprises, Inc. and Walden Media, LLC. All rights reserved.

Narnia.com

The Lion, the Witch and the Wardrobe: The Movie Storybook

Copyright © 2005 by C.S. Lewis Pte. Ltd.

The Chronicles of Narnia®, Narnia® and all book titles, characters and locales
original to The Chronicles of Narnia are trademarks of C.S. Lewis Pte. Ltd. Use without permission is strictly prohibited.

Photographs by Tony Barbera, Phil Bray, Richard Corman and Donald M. McAlpine.

Photos/illustration © 2005 Disney Enterprises, Inc. and Walden Media, LLC.

HarperCollins®, ®, and HarperEntertainment are trademarks of HarperCollins Publishers.

Library of Congress catalog card number: 2004117944.

Printed in the United States of America. For information address HarperCollins Children's Books,
a division of HarperCollins Publishers, 1350 Avenue of the Americas, New York, NY 10019.

Book design by Rick Farley

1 2 3 4 5 6 7 8 9 10

❖

First Edition

-THE CHRONICLES OF-
NARNIA
THE LION, THE WITCH AND THE WARDROBE

THE MOVIE STORYBOOK

Adapted by Kate Egan

Based on the screenplay
by Ann Peacock and Andrew Adamson
and Christopher Markus & Stephen McFeely

Based on the book by C. S. Lewis

Directed by Andrew Adamson

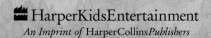

HarperKidsEntertainment
An Imprint of HarperCollinsPublishers

With air raids every night, wartime London was no place for children. So Mrs. Pevensie decided her four children would wait out the war in the countryside. "It's just for a little while," she promised as they boarded a train.

Peter, the oldest, looked at his sisters and brother. "We've got to stick together now," he said. Susan, Edmund and Lucy stared back at him glumly. Nobody wanted to go where they were going—wherever it was.

A stern woman named Mrs. Macready met them at the station. She worked for their host, Professor Kirke, and enforced all the rules at his huge, dark house. No shouting. No running. No sliding on the banisters. Life was quiet at the Professor's house. And deadly boring—especially on a rainy day.

Lucy suggested playing hide-and-seek. Peter had counted all the way up to ninety-six before she found a place to hide. In a rush, Lucy plunged into the magnificent wooden wardrobe that stood in a room of its own. She backed into it as far as she could go. Then suddenly she felt snow crunching beneath her feet!

Lucy was in the middle of a snow-covered forest! She made
her way through the icy trees, toward a faint light in the distance, and
found herself in a clearing beside a lamppost. Just when she was wondering
what to do next, she heard footsteps behind her. Lucy was being followed
by a creature who was half man, half goat. He was a Faun!

The Faun's name was Mr. Tumnus. It turned out he was more afraid of Lucy than Lucy was of him. And Lucy couldn't resist his invitation for tea—she was dying to get out of the cold. On the way to his house, Lucy discovered that she was in a land called Narnia, where it had been winter for the last one hundred years.

"Winter's all right," Lucy said, trying to sound cheerful. "You can ice skate and have snowball fights. And Christmas!"

Mr. Tumnus shook his head. "Not here," he replied sadly. "We haven't had Christmas for a hundred years."

Beside the Faun's blazing fire, Lucy ate all the tea cakes she could. But Mr. Tumnus seemed scared when she decided to leave. "If I let you go, she'll turn me to stone," he whispered. "The White Witch! She's the one who makes it always winter. She gave orders . . . if we ever find a Human in the woods, we're supposed to turn it over to her."

Mr. Tumnus broke the rules by helping her leave. Lucy just hoped he wouldn't get caught.

When she stepped back through the wardrobe, Lucy found that no time had passed at all. Nobody believed her story, either. That night, she crept down the hall with a candle and slipped back into Narnia. And this time Edmund followed her.

Edmund lost Lucy in the snow right away. But soon he met an elegant woman wrapped in fur, riding in a sleigh pulled by reindeer. She stopped when she saw him. "Pray, how did you come to enter my dominion?" she asked in an angry voice.

Nervously, Edmund stammered, "I-I-I'm not sure. . . . Lucy's the only one of us four who's been here before. . . . She said she met some Faun called T-T-Tumnus."

Suddenly the woman was friendlier. She conjured treats for Edmund—including his favorite, Turkish Delight! She told Edmund she was a Queen, and then she made him a tantalizing promise. One day, she might make him a Prince of Narnia—if only he would introduce her to his brother and sisters.

Edmund said good-bye to the nice Queen and watched her ride off in her sleigh. Moments later, he heard footsteps behind him. It was Lucy. "I told you Narnia was real!" she cried.

Lucy told him where she'd been. "I saw Mr. Tumnus," she explained. "He's fine. The White Witch hasn't found out anything about him meeting me." Edmund froze. He looked down at the sleigh tracks in the snow. "Are you all right?" Lucy asked. "You look awful."

"What do you expect? I'm freezing. How do we get out of here?"

To Peter and Susan, Edmund pretended there was no such thing as Narnia. Even when Lucy had cried and begged her siblings to believe her, Edmund still denied it. But then one day he accidentally hit a cricket ball through a window at the Professor's house. Mrs. Macready came running to check out the damage. The four kids were cornered—until they crammed into the wardrobe. When they wandered through the coats and felt the wet snow beneath their feet, everyone knew Lucy was telling the truth. "You little liar," Peter said to Edmund, threateningly.

The others hardly spoke to Edmund as they plodded through the
snow to visit Mr. Tumnus. But soon they had a bigger problem on their
hands. The Faun's house was ruined—and Mr. Tumnus was gone!

Lucy was sure it was her fault. What if Mr. Tumnus had been
turned to stone? She was determined to find him. Then two talking
Beavers appeared to help!

"There is hope, dear," Mrs. Beaver
assured her.

"There is more than hope," her husband
interrupted. "Aslan is on the move! He's the
King of the whole wood. He's the real King
of Narnia! And he's waiting for you at the
Stone Table!"

The Pevensies had no idea what he meant.

So the Beavers filled them in. Everything that was happening in Narnia—from Mr. Tumnus's arrest to Aslan's return—was because of them. An ancient prophecy dictated that when two Sons of Adam and two Daughters of Eve—also known as Human children—arrived in Narnia, Aslan would come back!

With him, they would lead an army against the White Witch and restore peace to the land. Then they would ascend to four thrones in a palace called Cair Paravel!

None of it made any sense to Susan. There were no such things as Witches. She didn't care to be a Queen. She just wanted to go home.

It was much too late to leave, though. While the Beavers were talking to them, Edmund had run away to join the White Witch!

Peter, Susan and Lucy ran after him until the Beavers set them straight. If they followed their brother, they would walk straight into the hands of the Witch—who was waiting to pounce. They would have to go directly to Aslan. He was the only one who could help Edmund now.

Lucy hated to abandon her brother. And it was an awfully long way to the Stone Table, over a frozen river and through a dense forest. Even worse, the Witch's Wolves were on their trail!

Suddenly she heard them. Lucy flew into the woods, diving after Peter, Susan and the Beavers into a small cave. Soon she could hear sleigh bells right outside. It had to be the Witch herself!

Mr. Beaver peeped out to get a look at her. But the Witch wasn't there. Instead it was Father Christmas, driving eight reindeer!

"I thought there was no Christmas in Narnia," said Susan suspiciously.

Father Christmas smiled. "Not for a long time," he said. "But the hope you have brought us, your Majesties, is finally weakening the Witch's magic. Still, you could probably do with these."

Father Christmas handed each of them
magnificent gifts.

Peter received a sword and a scabbard,
with a shield emblazoned with a lion.

Susan received a bow and a quiver
of arrows, plus an ivory horn. Father
Christmas promised that whenever she blew it,
help would come her way.

And Lucy received both a tiny dagger and a
jeweled vial containing the juice of the fireflower.
One drop of it would cure any injury.

Then Father Christmas flew
off across the snow, crying,
"Long live Aslan! And Merry
Christmas!" He was gone in
the blink of an eye.

Meanwhile, Edmund was in the Witch's clutches. There was no Turkish Delight for him at her castle. He wasn't about to become a Prince. Instead, the Witch was furious that Edmund had failed to deliver his brother and sisters. And she was angrier still when she found out they were looking for Aslan! If the children met up with the King, her reign would be in jeopardy. She would simply have to stop them!

The Witch strapped Edmund into her sleigh and went off in search of Peter, Susan and Lucy. She found the Fox who'd promised to guide them to the Stone Table—and she turned him into stone. Then the Witch ordered her Wolves to head off the children at the river.

Peter, Susan and Lucy had to get across the frozen river without the help of the Fox. It was hard to believe, but it seemed as if the river was beginning to melt.

Great cracks opened up in the ice as they
rushed across. And then they were ambushed by
the Witch's Wolves! The chief Wolf, Maugrim,
promised that Peter's family would be safe if only
they left Narnia at once. Peter wanted to believe
him. At the same time, though, other Wolves were
growling at the Beavers.

Peter didn't know what to do. He didn't like to
fight. He just wanted to have some peace.

Maugrim howled and prepared to tear him to pieces.

Just then, though, a waterfall above them gave way. Chunks of ice pounded the Wolves, and a torrent of water washed the children away!

When they landed on the shore of the river, shivering and wet, they all noticed a change in the air. They could actually feel the warm sun on their skin. Lucy pointed at the flowers popping out of the earth. Even Susan had to admit something miraculous was happening. Spring was coming to Narnia!

The White Witch had to
admit it, too. Her sleigh was
stuck in the mud! If she was ever
going to keep the Pevensies from
reaching Aslan, she would have to go on
foot. Wearily, Edmund trudged behind her.

The Beavers and the Pevensies made their way through the forest and came into a large clearing. There, a Centaur standing guard saw them and sounded a horn. A cluster of leaves swirled into the air, taking the form of a pair of Dryads who bowed to the children. As the party stepped forward, a magnificent sight sprawled before them—it was Aslan's camp.

The bustling creatures of the camp grew silent as the children and the Beavers moved through the crowd. There in the center of the camp was a huge tent. As they argued over who would go in first, the tent flap opened and the children fell silent, too. Before them stood a fearsome and beautiful golden Lion, his mane shimmering in the sun. It was Aslan.

Aslan welcomed the three children warmly. But then he asked, "Where is the fourth?"

The Pevensies explained how Edmund had betrayed them to the Witch, how they loved him anyway because he was their brother and how they needed Aslan's help if they were ever to find him.

Aslan listened carefully and said, "All shall be done for Edmund."

Later, Peter took a walk alone with Aslan. The Lion showed him Cair Paravel, glittering in the distance, where someday he was to sit as the High King.

Peter wasn't sure he could do it. He wasn't even sure he wanted to. He'd had a hard enough time keeping his family safe. How could he ever be a King?

Aslan said, "Peter, I will do all I can to help your family. But I need you to consider what I ask of you." He pointed at his bustling camp and added, "I, too, want my family safe."

If he was ever to deliver Edmund from the Witch's grasp, Peter would have to deliver Narnia from her grasp, too. He would have to help fight her forces. He would have to fulfill the prophecy.

Suddenly Wolves sneaked up on Susan and Lucy, who were bathing in a river. A Centaur, Oreius, rushed to help the girls—until Aslan stopped him. "No, Oreius, let the young Prince fight this battle," he said.

This time Peter drew his sword without hesitating. This time he fought— both for Narnia and for Edmund. And this time Maugrim was killed.

That night Centaurs slipped into the Witch's camp and rescued Edmund. Aslan brought him to the other children at dawn, instructing, "There is no need to speak to Edmund about what is past." They weren't quite ready to forgive their brother, but nobody dared to defy Aslan.

Now that they were all together, Susan wanted to go home. After all, she pointed out, this was a war just like the one their mother wanted to protect them from. But Peter knew what he had to do now. And Edmund understood the Witch's strength. The four of them would have to fight her forces. They would have to get ready for battle.

Then they learned that Aslan had agreed to meet with the Witch. She arrived in a procession of monsters and snarled, "You have a traitor amongst you, Aslan. And every traitor belongs to me."

Aslan and the Witch spoke alone. When they were through, Aslan announced to the crowd, "She has renounced her claim on Edmund's blood." He sealed the deal with a mighty roar, and the Witch marched away.

War still loomed, but Edmund was safe.

That night, Lucy was lying awake when she saw Aslan's shadow move past her tent. She and Susan followed him to the Stone Table, which was lit by torches and surrounded by the Witch and her monsters. They taunted and tormented the Lion. They teased and poked him. And then they killed him! Susan and Lucy could hardly believe their eyes.

Back in the camp, Peter heard the terrible news. Now it seemed impossible for him to do what Aslan had asked.

But Edmund encouraged him. "Aslan chose you to lead his army," he reminded his brother. "That army is ready to follow you. And so am I!"

Suddenly Peter felt a little braver. "Tell the troops that we will meet the Witch in battle without Aslan," he commanded Oreius.

On a white Unicorn, Peter headed for the battlefield.

At the sound of a trumpet, the Witch's army stormed onto the field. It was a teeming mass of all the evil creatures known to Narnia. Peter's army was completely outnumbered.

Peter rode to the front of his troops and took a deep breath. The army was attentive—but silent. "For Narnia! For Aslan!" he cried. The troops exploded into applause, clanging their swords against their shields.

And Peter led the charge toward the Witch's army!

Susan and Lucy were grief stricken. They couldn't bear to leave Aslan's body even if the battle was beginning. But suddenly they heard a strange rumbling, and then a sound like thunder and an earthquake all at once. When the shaking subsided, they found that the Stone Table had been split in two . . . and Aslan himself stood before them!

The Witch's magic was powerful, he explained. But there was something more powerful than even she knew: the difference between right and wrong. When a Narnian created as much wrong as the Witch did, even death could be overturned!

The girls climbed on Aslan's back and galloped across the countryside to the melting ruins of the Witch's ice castle. In the courtyard they found the stone statues the Witch had created with her dark magic—and one of them was Mr. Tumnus! Aslan breathed on the Faun until he came back to life. The Lion did the same for the thousands of other statues. Then he led them back to the battlefield—and not a moment too soon.

Peter's army was on the verge of collapse. The Witch had turned many of his soldiers to stone. She was now closing in on Peter, her wand raised. Seeing this, Edmund brought down his sword and smashed the wand in two. Furious, the White Witch let out a horrible scream. She wounded Edmund with what was left of her wand and he fell to the ground.

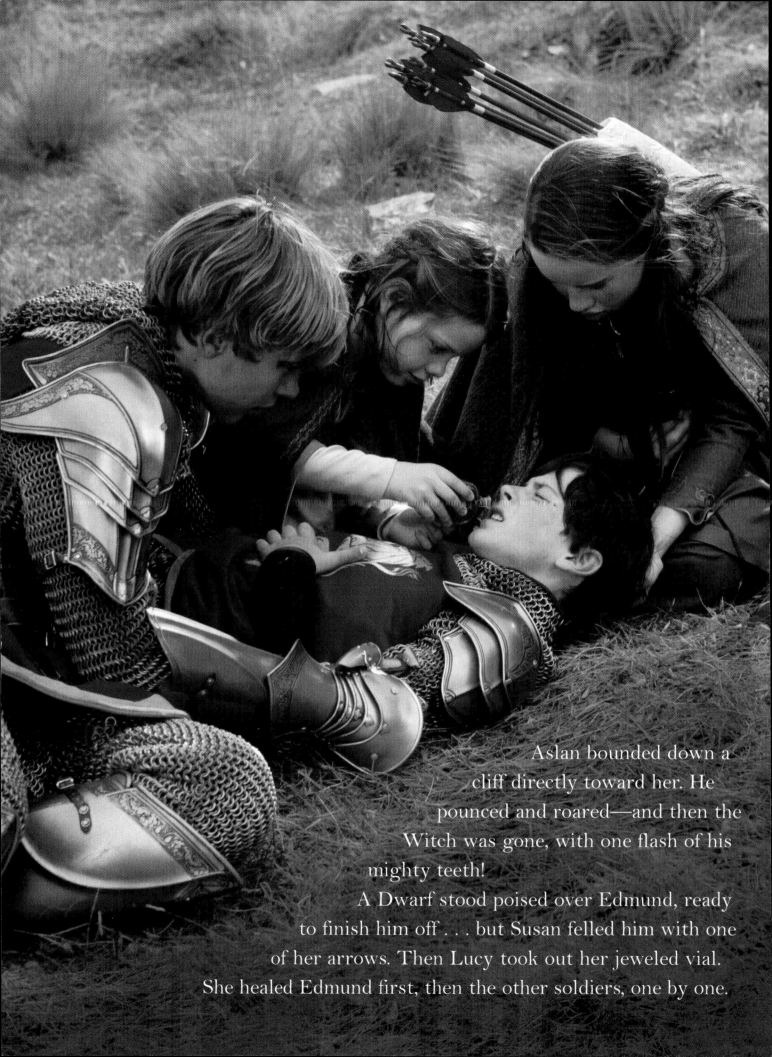

Aslan bounded down a
cliff directly toward her. He
pounced and roared—and then the
Witch was gone, with one flash of his
mighty teeth!
A Dwarf stood poised over Edmund, ready
to finish him off . . . but Susan felled him with one
of her arrows. Then Lucy took out her jeweled vial.
She healed Edmund first, then the other soldiers, one by one.

Their work on the battlefield was done. Now it was time for the Pevensies to be crowned at Cair Paravel!

Peter, Susan, Edmund and Lucy sat upon their new thrones and beamed as Aslan pronounced them the new Kings and Queens of Narnia. A great celebration began in the ancient castle . . . and only Lucy noticed the Lion slipping away.

Fifteen years later, the Kings and Queens set off in search of the famous White Stag. They tore off after it into the woods until the branches gave way and they found themselves . . . in a wardrobe.

They realized no time at all had passed since they entered the wardrobe. The Kings and Queens were children again, back inside the Professor's house.

That night Lucy crept back to the room with the wardrobe.

Suddenly she heard a sound. She wheeled around and found the Professor there, shaking his head. "I'm afraid you won't get back in that way. I already tried."

"Will we ever go back?" Lucy asked sadly.

And the Professor answered, "I should think so. But it'll likely happen when you're not looking for it. All the same . . . best to keep your eyes open."